ALIYA OLA

PATAIL

Volume two of Disney Princess Classic Library

Printed in China

First Edition
1 3 5 7 9 10 8 6 4 2

T425-2382-5-12288
ISBN 978-1-4231-8091-3
For more Disney Press fun, visit www.disneybooks.com
This book was printed on paper created from a sustainable source.

Aurora and the Helpful Dragon

𝒟ISNEY PRESS

New York

"I'LL RACE YOU TO THE LOOKOUT POINT!" Princess Aurora called to Prince Phillip as they galloped through the forest one sunny fall morning. She sped away on her horse, Moonlight, with Prince Phillip close behind.

Just as Aurora and Phillip rounded a bend, they heard a funny noise. A small dragon popped out from behind a tree and scampered toward Aurora.

"Oh, he's so cute!" Aurora exclaimed as she dismounted.

"Grrgrrgrr?" the little dragon murmured, clambering into Aurora's lap.

But Phillip was worried. "Dragons can be dangerous!"

The little dragon shook his head no.

"I think he's saying he's not dangerous," Aurora laughed. "Please, let's take him home. I'm going to name him Crackle!"

"He does seem like a harmless little fellow," Phillip agreed.

But Moonlight was still afraid. She tossed her mane and pawed the ground. Crackle's tail drooped sadly. Then he grinned a funny little grin. Suddenly, he licked Moonlight's nose with his long, warm tongue. Moonlight blinked with surprise and nuzzled Crackle under the chin. The little dragon giggled.

"Moonlight likes Crackle!" Aurora said happily.

When Phillip and Aurora rode into the courtyard, the three fairies were hanging banners for King Stefan and the Queen, who were coming for a ball that night.

Flora gasped when she saw Crackle. "Dragons can be dangerous," she said.

"Remember the last one!" Fauna added.

"Oooh, I think he's sweet," Merryweather spoke up.

"Grrrgrr," Crackle babbled.

"He thinks you're sweet, too," Aurora told Merryweather as Prince Phillip swept his princess across the courtyard.

Just then, Crackle noticed a kitten in Fauna's workbasket.

Crackle listened to the cute kitten purring. Then he scrunched up his mouth and closed his eyes.

"Purrgrr, purrgrr!" Crackle tried to purr. Clouds of smoke puffed from his nose and mouth.

"Aachoo! Aachooooie! Ah-ah-ah-CHOO!" The fairies sneezed so hard that they fluttered backward.

"Please—*Achoo!*—stop trying to purr!" Fauna exclaimed.

Crackle looked sad for a moment. Then he saw the kitten playing with a ball of yarn from the workbasket, and his eyes lit up. He snatched a ball of yarn with his mouth. *Whoosh!*—it caught fire. Merryweather put the fire out with her wand.

"Oh, Crackle," Aurora said gently. "You're not a kitten. You're a dragon." Crackle's lower lip trembled.

Just then, Crackle saw Phillip leading the horses into the stables. A dog followed Phillip, barking and wagging its tail. Crackle wagged his tail and ran to the stables, too.

"Woofgrr, woofgrr," he tried to bark. Flames shot from his mouth and caught some straw on fire. Phillip poured water on the burning straw.

"You're not a dog," he said kindly, shooing Crackle away.

Aurora carried Crackle into the castle and cuddled him on a window seat. A bird was singing outside. Crackle's ears perked up and his eyes shone hopefully.

"LAAAlaagrr!" he bellowed.

King Hubert heard the racket and rushed into the room.

"Oh, my, my, my! How did a dragon get in here?" he blustered.

Frightened by the king, Crackle jumped from the window seat and ran into the garden. Aurora ran after him. She found the little dragon sitting beside a fountain. Crackle was studying a fish swimming in the lower pool.

Before Aurora could stop him, Crackle splashed into the water. The startled fish leaped into the higher pool.

"Crackle, you're not a fish!" Aurora exclaimed. "You're not a kitten or a dog or a bird, either. You're a dragon!"

Tears rolled down Crackle's face. "Grrgrrgrr," he sobbed.

Suddenly, Aurora understood.

"Do you think no one will like you because you're a dragon?" she asked.

Crackle nodded and whimpered sadly.

"Crackle, you can't change being a dragon," Aurora said kindly. "But you don't have to be a dangerous dragon. You can be a brave, helpful dragon."

Crackle stopped crying. "Grrgrrgrrgrr?" he growled.

Before Aurora could answer, thunder boomed. Wind blew black clouds over the sun. Aurora snatched up Crackle. She reached the castle doors just as the rain began to pour down.

Everyone was gathered in the grand hallway, watching the storm.

"I'm afraid King Stefan and the Queen might lose their way on the road above the cliffs," Prince Phillip said, his voice filled with concern. "I should ride out to help."

Aurora looked at Crackle. "Do you want to show everyone that you're a brave and helpful dragon?" she asked.

"GRRRgrrrgrr!" Crackle exclaimed enthusiastically.

"Fly to the top of the highest castle tower," Aurora explained. "Then blow the largest, brightest flames you can."

Aurora watched Crackle as the little fellow soared upward.

"Come on, everyone!" the princess called. She ran to get a better view of the watchtower. Phillip and the others followed close behind.

Everyone tried to see Crackle at the top of the tower, but the storm was too dark and strong. Suddenly, they saw huge flames. They were coming from little Crackle! Gold and red light flashed up into the sky above the watchtower.

Again and again, Crackle blew his flames until, at last, Phillip shouted, "I see King Stefan and the Queen! They're almost here!"

Everyone hurried to greet the visiting royals.

"The tower light saved us!" King Stefan exclaimed. "I need one like it!"

At that moment Crackle happily flew down to join in the fun.

"Well, there he is! Our new tower light," King Hubert said with a laugh.

"A dragon?" King Stefan asked. "But dragons are danger—"

"Not Crackle," Aurora interrupted. "He's a brave and helpful dragon!"

That night at the ball, Crackle lit the candles, warmed the food, and kept the fireplace blazing. King Hubert and the fairies were so pleased that they took turns scratching Crackle beneath his chin.

As Prince Phillip and Aurora danced, Crackle trotted beside them. Outside, it was cold and stormy. But inside, everyone was happy and warm—especially Crackle, the helpful dragon.

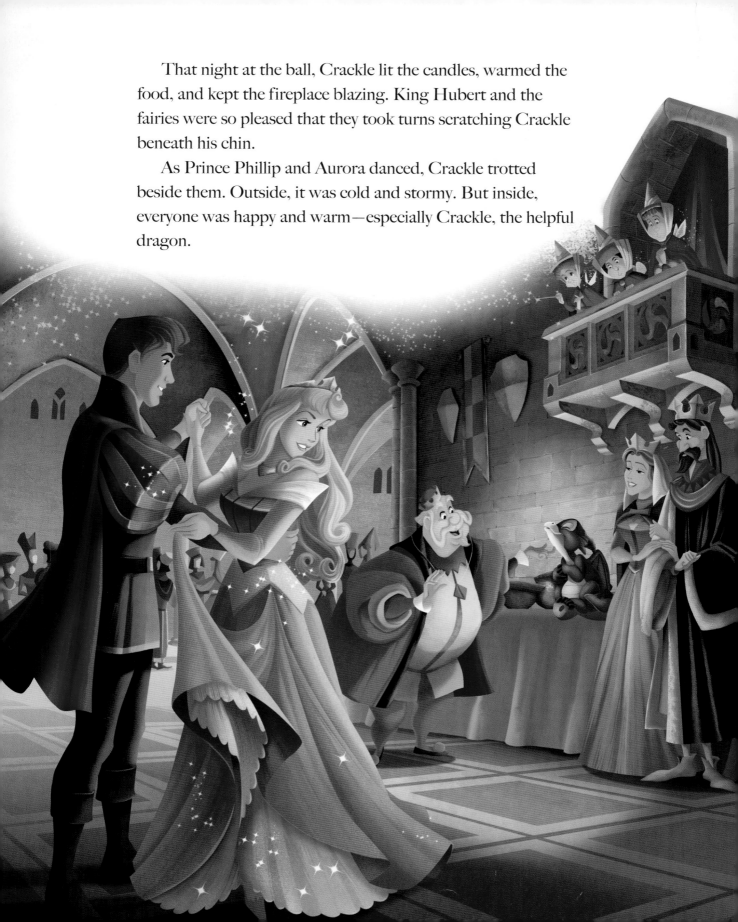